UP IN THE CLOUDS....

HOW OLD ARE YOU ANYWAY?
I'M A SOLID FOUR DAYS OLD THANK YOU VERY MUCH.
OH MAN! YOU'RE A DAY OLDER THAN ME AND YOU STILL LOOK LIKE A BABY!
LOOK AT HIM HE'S SO SMALL! HAHAHAHA.

HEY!
MY DAD WAS IN THE LAST OPERATION AND HE TAUGHT ME EVERYTHING HE KNEW.
SO HE TAUGHT YOU HOW TO LOOK LIKE A BABY? HAHAHAA.

BACK OFF MEANIE, PICK ON SOMEONE YOUR OWN SIZE.
OWN SIZE??
OKAY, LET ME GO FIND TEN MORE GUYS AND THEN WE'LL PICK ON YOU TOO!
THEY'RE BULLIES, DON'T WORRY ABOUT THEM JUNIOR.
MAYBE THEY'RE RIGHT, I'M TOO SMALL.

AND I'M TOO BIG, BUT LIKE MY DAD USED TO TELL ME: THE BIGGER THE TUMMY, THE BIGGER THE SPLASH!
YOU SURE ABOUT THAT?

NO DOUBT ABOUT IT!

LATER THAT DAY....
HOW WAS YOUR DAY MY CUTE LITTLE DROPLET? YOU LOOK SAD...
SOME OTHER RAINDROPS SAID I LOOK LIKE A BABY AND I'M TOO SMALL.
DON'T LET THOSE RAINDROPS DROWN YOU WITH CRITICISM, DEAR. IF YOU WANT TO GET BIG YOU JUST HAVE TO EAT MORE CLOUDS.
EWWW YOU KNOW I HATE EATING CLOUDS; THEY'RE SO FILLING AND HAVE ZERO FLAVOR.
YUUUUCK.
PTUI!

THEN IT NEEDS MORE SALT. EVERYTHING'S BETTER WITH MORE SALT!
THANKS MOM.

TRAINING DAY....

I'M UP FIRST CUZ I'M NUMBER ONE, GET IT - FIRST TO GO CUZ I'M FIRST PLACE.
OHHH YEAH!
JUST DROP.

YEAH, FIRST PLACE IN ANNOYING.
SEE YOU AT THE BOTTOM CRY-BABIES!

SPLASH!

YEAH THAT'S RIGHT! I BET YOU'RE ANNOYED BY THAT AMAZING JUMP!
HAHAHAH!
COME ON JUNIOR. REMEMBER JUST STICK OUT YOUR TUMMY. LET IT ALL HANG OUT, LIKE THIS.

ERRR...
BOOP!
OKAY...
HERE GOES NOTHING...

JUMP ALREADY!

YOUR TUMMY JUNIOR, PUFF OUT YOUR TUMMY!

BOOP!

NO WAY!!
HE CHEATED, HE MUST'VE CHEATED!

THAT WAS A PERFECT TUMMY PUFF! YOU CAN'T CHEAT THAT KIND OF THING.
TALK TO THE HAND.
I DID IT... I ACTUALLY DID IT.

ALL RIGHT YOU SCAREDY-DROPS!
IF THE LITTLE TWERP CAN DO IT SO CAN YOU! LET'S GO!

SEE GUYS, IT'S ALL ABOUT THE TUMMY.

DAY OF THE DROP....
ALL RIGHT YOU WET, FILTHY, SEWAGE H2O'S, ARE YOU READY TO RAIN!?
YES SIR!
YES SIR!
YES SIR!

I CAN'T HEAR YOU!
SIR, YES SIR!!

THAT'S WHAT I LIKE TO HEAR DROPLETS!
LISTEN TO ME WHEN I SAY THIS...
...WE WILL RAIN DOWN ON THE DIRT BELOW...

OH MAN, GENERAL DROP'S SPEECHES ARE LEGENDARY.

...WE WILL STORM THE BEACHES WITH THE UTMOST FORCE...
YOU GETTING CHILLS TOO? JEEZ I MIGHT JUST HAIL.

...AND TOGETHER WE WILL ACHIEVE TOTAL TORRENTIAL DOWNPOUR!
NOW LET'S RAIN DOWN AND CLEANSE THE EARTH OF ITS SINS!
WOOHOO!!

GOOD LUCK JUNIOR AND REMEMBER, TUMMY OUT.
TUMMY OUT.
HEY, WILL I EVER SEE YOU AGAIN?

WELL, LEGEND HAS IT...
...IF YOU'RE LUCKY, THE HEAVENLY SUN MAY JUST LIFT YOU BACK INTO THE CLOUDS, BUT IF YOU ASK ME, I THINK IT'S JUST A BUNCH OF MUMBO JUMBO.
MUMBO JUMBO?

MUM-BO JUM-BO. JUST SAYING IT MAKES YOU FEEL GOOD. TRY IT.
MUM-BO JUM-BO.
YOU GOT IT LITTLE BUDDY. HEY, YOU WANT TO RACE TO THE BOTTOM?
YEAH, LET'S DO IT.

ALL RIGHT, SEE YOU AT THE BOTTOM!
MUMBO JUMBO!!

HERE GOES NOTHING...

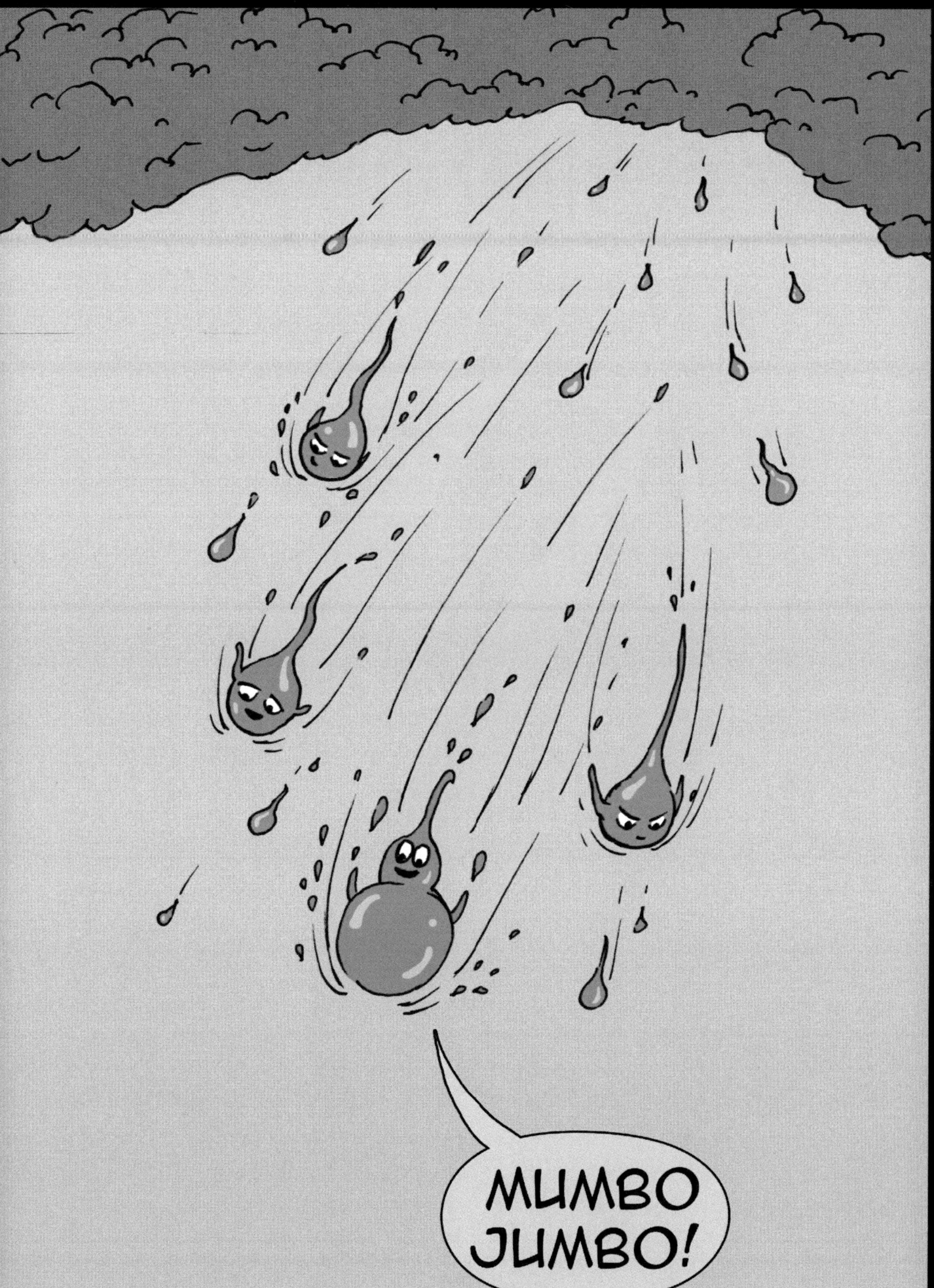

THE END.

Made in the USA
Middletown, DE
06 February 2021

32528286R00018